"I'm outta here, Boss!"

DISAPPEARING INC.

DAKOTA KING
AGENT AT LARGE

Hi Boss,
  Just in case you get
tired of watching TV reruns,
here's something to fool
around with. This is the
OPERATION BLACK FANG file
I put together.
  I've given you all the
facts and clues. All you
and the gang have to
do is piece it all
together and solve the
case. If you need any
help, forget it. I'm off to
the jungle.
      I'm outta here, Boss!

DK

THE SECRET FILES OF
DAKOTA KING

#1 Operation Black Fang

Jake MacKenzie

SCHOLASTIC INC.
New York Toronto London Auckland Sydney

Design and Illustration: **Hal Aber**

Cover Illustration: **Bill Purdom**

Photographs: **Neal Edwards**

Scholastic Books are available at special discounts for quantity purchases for use as premiums, promotional items, retail sales through specialty market outlets, etc. For details contact: Special Sales Manager, Scholastic Inc., 730 Broadway, New York, NY 10003.

ISBN 0-590-40749-X

12 11 10 9 8 7 6 5 4 3 2 1   7 8 9/8 0 1 2/9
                                                  28

Printed in the U.S.A
First Scholastic printing, September 1987

ZONE OPERATIONS ORGANIZATION

9009 Incognito Drive Arlington, Virginia 90909

703·555·9009   TELEX: 99-9009

MEMORANDUM

TO: All agents in the Z.O.O. (Zone Operations Organization)

FROM: The Zookeeper

CONCERNING: The Dakota King File

<u>OPERATION BLACK FANG</u>

Once again Dakota King has skipped out and left the Organization holding the bag. And once again, his usual parting words were "I'm outta here, Boss." Disappearing Inc. is the perfect name for an agency run by a guy like that. When last seen, he was parachuting into the interior of Brazil with his companion and survival trainer, Inc. agent, Longh Gonh. Our satellite tracking beam managed to follow him halfway up the Amazon River before we lost him. He probably pulled his old trick of strapping his tracking device to the leg of a bird and setting it loose.

He left us a small waterproof canvas satchel. Inside was the biggest mess of papers you'd ever want to see:

ratty newspaper clippings, some police reports I can barely make head or tail out of, what appear to be transcripts of DK's personal tape-recorded diary, drawings, a torn label, and so on. Looks as if he emptied his wastepaper basket and sent it to me.

Knowing DK, there is probably more to this than just a bunch of clippings. If this case is anything like that episode in the Far East, he's probably on to something. But, as usual, he was simply too restless to hang around and finish up the work. The only solid information DK gave me about this mess of clues is the note he attached to the file.

Since I don't have the time to work on this by myself, I'm sending this dossier to all agents. THAT MEANS YOU! Copies of everything DK sent me are here. What I want you to do is read it all and figure out who committed the crime.

I've included Dakota's profile and my instructions in the file which follows.

Good luck, agents — you'll need it!

The Zookeeper

ZONE OPERATIONS ORGANIZATION

CONFIDENTIAL PROFILE REPORT

Subject: Dakota King

Age: Unrecorded

Height: 6′ 3″

Distinguishing marks: Eagle tattoo on inside of left wrist

Address: General Post Office Every Major City

Home Base: Redd Cliff, Colorado

Contact Base: The Z.O.O.

Partner and Contact: Longh Gonh (separate profile on file), Disappearing Inc. agent

Occupation: Agent-at-large for own agency, Disappearing Inc.

Services valued by Organization: Investigative skills used in studies of unexplained events, uncharted territories, unsolved mysteries of the world.

Special Interests: Freedom and justice for all—especially Dakota King; fine art and illustration (published works of Dakota King's own art include: Dakota King's Sketchbook, King's Ransom: Collected Drawings of Dakota King, and Dakota!); magic (King is a world-renowned magician known for contributing numerous tricks and illusions to master magicians on all continents).

Education: Life experience. Spent boyhood traveling with anthropologist parents who found him living with the Kayuga Indians in Death Valley and adopted him when he was a small boy. Travels exposed him to numerous tribal cultures in this country and all over the world.

While living with the Kayuga he received survival training, learned to read nature's danger signals, learned to use the celestial bodies, the oceans, rivers, and earth's vibrations as means of predicting events and even changing events. Acclaimed expert in the customs and mystical ceremonies of American Indian tribes. Followed and lived with Gypsy tribes in Hungary, Italy, and throughout Europe. Accepted and welcomed by all Gypsy tribes on every continent as adopted son of Zolan, King of the Gypsies. No stranger to the Himalayas and the unnumbered villages and unchartered regions which lay hidden on the summits, in the valleys, and in the caves of these mysterious mountains. Recognized expert in knowledge of great impostors of the 18th, 19th, and 20th centuries.

Experience: Consultant to government intelligence agencies in the use of illusions for diversion tactics to be used as alternatives to weapons. References available on request from members of the private sector who have used his services for finding lost treasures and tracing family fortunes.

Hobbies: Flying, race car driving, D & D, art, inventing communication devices, and experiencing life.

Light Plane Goes Down in Mountains

No Survivors Found at Crash Site

By Deirdre Corey

Gila Bend Gazette

GILA BEND, UT, June 30 — A small plane crashed at the base of the Razor Ridge mountains late this afternoon leaving no known survivors but plenty of questions.

Forest ranger Rick Stapnick saw the single-engine craft descend towards the forest at the foot of the mountains and disappear into the treetops. He sounded the alarm to the Rescue Service who dispatched a helicopter crew to the site.

When rescuers arrived, they found the plane still largely intact and several footprints around the site. An extensive search of the area failed to turn up any survivors—dead or alive.

A check of ownership traced the airplane back to Getaway Plane Rental 200 miles away. A check of the records showed that the craft had been rented by a Mr. Sherman Woosner of Hathaway Park. There is apparently no such person at that address. Police are still investigating.

PHOTO: THOMAS A. HORNE

Mysterious crash baffles police.

Dakota King's
Microdiary Entry #1
Re: Operation Black Fang

    I've got to admit even the guys in Operations Science Intelligence were impressed when I showed them this recorder in my wristwatch. Another little invention of mine that has come in handy, especially lately. I can store about two days' worth of information on these quarter-sized discs. I use it for my personal diary and for recording conversations—secretly, of course. Sure beats taking notes or dragging around a tape recorder.

    Longh Gonh and I were into our third day of escape and evasion exercise in the foothills of Gila Bend, Utah when we saw a plane go down. Longh had been pushing me hard all day, trying to get me in shape for our upcoming jungle trip. I had been taking it easy after our wild adventure in the Far East, and I was out of shape. But Disappearing Inc., my freelance adventure agency, is a business, not a hobby. And when a client calls with a big job to do, like the one in South America we were training for, it's time to lay off the easy life and start training. No better trainer than Longh Gonh when it's time to toughen up. The guy's got the endurance of a camel and the strength of two elephants, but the speed and lightness of an antelope. Not to mention the fact that the government hires him to train drill sergeants. He's worth three times the salary I pay him.

On this jungle-training mission, though, I was tempted to fire the guy. He never let up. "Five more miles! No more water! No rations until sundown!" I'd been listening to that for days, and I was tired of it.

Longh, on the other hand, never seemed to tire. "I'm not going any farther today!" I yelled.

As usual, he ignored me. "You will continue, Dakota," he said calmly. Well, Longh was wrong; we noticed something odd that stopped us right where we were—a surprise from the sky. Planes of all kinds had been passing overhead now and again, and we had pretty much ignored them. But the last one was different. At first I couldn't put my finger on why, but after a couple more seconds of concentration I realized what was so strange.

The plane was gradually nosing lower, as though it were going to land. But where? The nearest airport was over a hundred fifty miles away. Slowly the light plane dipped down from the sky. It swooped overhead and went gliding straight into a hill about a hundred yards ahead of us.

Longh and I scrambled through the brush. When we got there, we saw that the plane had hit a particularly dense cluster of trees, which cushioned its landing like a large pillow. The wings were mostly ripped off, but the cockpit was intact. Maybe the pilot and passengers, if any, had survived.

Pushing our way through the broken trees, we reached the plane. Longh pulled out his first aid kit as I ran ahead. The cockpit door was jammed shut. After some heavy tugging, I managed to drag it open. When I looked inside I found that no one had survived the crash.

Because there was no one there.

"There are no passengers and no pilot, Longh!" I

said in disbelief.

"That is not possible. There must be someone, Dakota," Longh replied.

"Well, take a look."

Longh looked into the cockpit. Empty.

"You are correct Dakota. It does not make sense, but there it is." He wore his look of intense concentration.

"You know what we have just seen?" I demanded, hoping to see Longh get as excited as I was.

"A plane crash," he answered calmly.

"Think a little harder, Longh. A plane has crashed before our eyes with no pilot, no passengers. Nothing. And no signs of anyone having been thrown clear," I summed up.

Then as we tried to figure out this mystery, I spotted something on the floor of the plane. A **long stick with a Y-shaped crotch at the end** lay near the plane's controls. "Now, what the . . ." I began. And then I knew. "I've got it!" I cried out, handing the stick to Longh.

Longh always seems to know what I'm thinking, sometimes even before I say it—another thing I pay him for. I watched as he propped the forked end of the stick so it wedged the plane's joystick in position. "This functioned as a crude but effective automatic pilot," he said.

The plane was an old clunker and too out-of-date to have a real automatic pilot. It looked as if someone had wedged the stick under the controls so the plane would nosedive and crash. Looking behind the seat, I found a clue as to how the human pilot had managed all of this. Lying on the floor was a neat, tightly packed bundle of a **reserve parachute, the kind paratroopers and skydivers usually carry strapped to their chest in case the main chute doesn't open.** Whoever it was had enough confidence in his main chute not to need his backup. It would

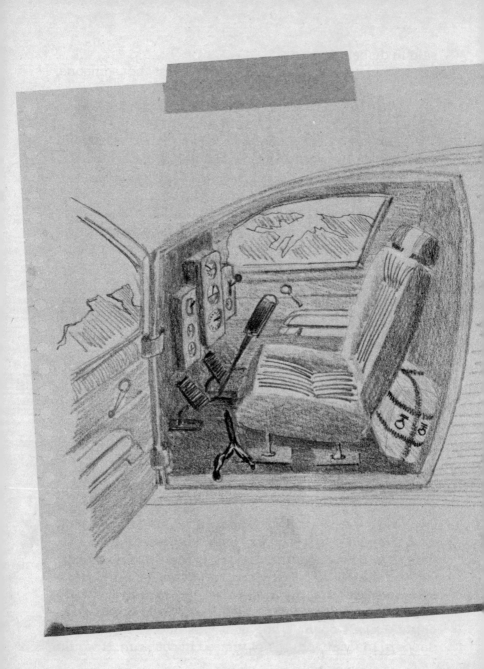

have been a simple matter to use it to wedge the stick under the controls and jump out before the plane went down.

What Longh and I couldn't figure out was how and why someone would abandon a perfectly flying plane. The fuel gauge showed plenty of gas.

Just then a glimmer of something red caught my eye. It was a **scrap of red paper** caught in the frame of the seat.

CLUE #1

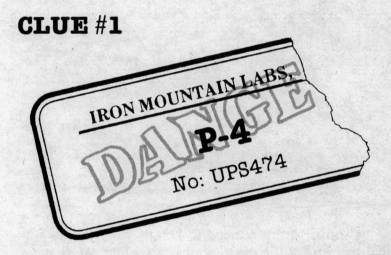

I picked up the scrap and tucked it into my backpack. At the same time I pulled out my sketchpad and did a quick drawing of the crash scene—the broken trees, the plane, even the **left-handed glove** stuck in the door. Never know how things might change after Longh and I went back to base camp.

CLUE #2

"I think," I announced to Longh, "my jungle survival training will have to wait for a while. We've got a case to solve right here."

The fastest route back to our rendezvous point with our helicopter was a day's climb straight up a sheer cliff. Longh was only too happy to find this wall of rock. "My mother's Indian blood makes my heart cry out for such heights," he said, looking up at the hundreds of feet of rock. "And my father's Oriental blood lets me face such a challenge with serenity," he said, scaling the rock face with the ease of a spider.

Well, I don't have any Indian blood or Oriental serenity. But thanks to my mother and father I know a lot of what they know. My parents were famous anthropologists. They traveled around the world studying the lost arts and skills of primitive peoples. They had a special system for studying the secret ways of the tribes and villages. Instead of asking a medicine man or village chief outright how he worked his magic or was able to survive weeks in the desert without carrying food and water, they asked the natives to teach me how they did it. And once I learned, I passed the information on to my mother and father.

I spent much of my early boyhood with the Kayuga Indians in Death Valley where I learned Indian skills: finding my way in the dark by the stars; tracking animals across rock; traveling fifty miles a day across the most brutal desert conditions in the world; finding water by smell. And, most of all, learning to use my eyes to see all there was to see and my ears to hear every sound. Years later, when we moved to the Orient, I learned some of the martial arts and the Ways of the Master.

While I stood lost in thoughts of my childhood, Longh used the free time to make like a mountain lion. There he was, a small dot against the sky at the top of the cliff, while I was down in the brush trying to figure out our chances of being airlifted to the top.

"Mountains grow no smaller as time grows shorter!" Longh yelled down, each word echoing down the mountain walls.

"You can say that again," I muttered to myself as I hauled my tired body up slowly but surely. "You can say that again," the rock walls softly echoed back.

Dakota King's
Microdiary Entry #2
Re: Operation Black Fang

The next day, the sight of the helicopter landing at the summit was a welcome one. Wings Atkins, the pilot, greeted us with a newspaper in hand. "Hey, guys, you were practically standing on top of yesterday's biggest news story. A plane went down right around here somewhere!" Wings handed me the paper. Longh and I looked at each other. I could sense just by his face that he was wondering if we should say anything to Wings about our visit to the wreck. Without my speaking a word, Longh read the answer in my eyes: No. The crash was something we wanted to investigate unofficially, on our own.

The flight back to our base camp gave us a chance to relax a little. When we landed at the camp, I ran, not walked, right to the food supply and threw a thick steak on the fire—sensing Longh's disapproval. He's strictly a vegetarian. What else!

After dinner I sat there and laid my sketch of the plane wreck and the scrap of red paper out in front of me. I reread the follow-up plane crash story in the newspaper. There wasn't much there. It mentioned that some patrol team had found a lot of footprints, but I knew those were ours, so that was no help. Tracking down the plane's registration didn't help either. It was rented at Johnnycake Airport, a small airfield about two hundred miles from the crash site. Whoever rented the plane had vanished. According to the paper, a plane ticket and threatening note were sent to the rental agent, who was last seen flying toward South America. The article included a photo of the plane wreckage and a **picture of the threatening note:**

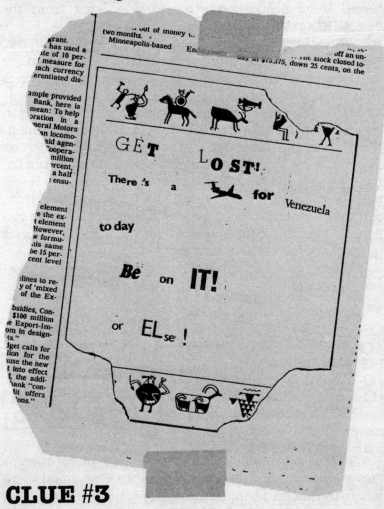

CLUE #3

With no witnesses, that left us with just one clue, the scrap of red paper found inside the plane. It didn't take a lot of deep thinking to tell where it came from: Iron Mountain Laboratory, a government research center located in Death Valley, California. It was rumored that all kinds of strange experiments were going on there, some of them pretty risky judging from the "DANGE" on the torn label.

When I got back to my temporary training outpost, I sat down in front of my computer and hooked into my network of computer renegades. I knew from previous experience that only the smartest, nosiest renegade would do. So I left a message on the electronic bulletin board for Zan (short for Alexandra) and then had lunch. She goes by the name Zan and so I made Tarzan my code name. I've never met her, but she's been doing favors for me for years. Somehow—I never ask—she is able to get me information on anyone in the United States: from someone's dental record to how much money a person has in his checking account. As payment, I deposit money into her electronic account.

When I checked my monitor later, there was a message waiting for me:

TARZAN: MIDNIGHT AT MY PLACE. DON'T FORGET TO BRING FLOWERS.

It was a simple kind of code. "My place" meant Zan's private computer access number. She would leave her machine on at midnight and wait for my call. The

"Bring flowers" was another part of the code. To make sure I was the one who was calling, we had worked out a special password system: I would "draw" seven flowers on her computer screen like so:

❀❀❁❀❀❀❀

Each flower stem stood for a day in the week. When I drew them I would leave "the bud" off of one. The one without the bud marked the day of the week I was contacting her. Since I was calling on a Tuesday I left the bud off the third flower. It was all necessary, said Zan. There were "certain people" (she never said who) who would like to see her out of business. And since I wanted her to stay in business, I played by her rules.

Midnight came. I clicked on my computer and typed my "flowers" across the screen:

❀❀❁❀❀❀❀

I waited. Nothing happened.

I typed them again. Bright glowing letters appeared on my screen.

COMPUTER CONVERSATION

● HELLO HANDSOME, THANKS FOR THE BOUQUET.

● ANYTIME, ZAN.

● WHAT'S YOUR PROBLEM, HONEY?

● TELL ME WHAT YOU KNOW ABOUT A PLACE CALLED IRON MOUNTAIN LAB.

- NOT A GREAT PLACE FOR A DATE. COULDN'T YOU SUGGEST SOMEWHERE A LITTLE MORE ROMANTIC? PARIS? ROME?
- GET SERIOUS, ZAN. WHAT DO THEY DO THERE?
- DOOMSDAY BUG. GOVERNMENT SCIENTISTS ARE TRYING TO MAKE NEW AND BETTER POISONS. IT'S PART OF SOME BIG HUSH-HUSH PROJECT TO MAKE KILLER GERMS FOR FIGHTING BATTLES WITH DISEASES, NOT BULLETS.
- HOW DO YOU FIGHT A BATTLE WITH DISEASES?
- EASY. YOU VACCINATE YOUR OWN SOLDIERS AGAINST ONE OF YOUR OWN CUSTOM-MADE GERMS, THEN SPRAY THE GERMS ALL OVER THE BAD GUYS, LIKE A CROP DUSTER SPRAYS PLANTS. IN A FEW DAYS, THE COMPETITION IS REAL SICK. YOUR TROOPS WALK IN AND—TA DA!—VICTORY.
- OK. BUT ANOTHER THING: THERE WAS A LABEL WE FOUND FROM THE LAB. ON IT WAS SOME WRITING.

LIKE WHAT?

IN BIG BLACK MARKINGS WAS: **P-4.**

P-4!!!! YOU SURE?

- POSITIVE. WHY?
- **P-4** DESIGNATES ONLY THE MOST DANGER-OUS DRUGS AND CHEMICALS. THOSE THINGS ARE USUALLY KEPT IN AIRTIGHT LABS AND WORKED ON BY SCIENTISTS WEARING GERM-PROOF SPACESUITS. GET ONE OF THOSE BUGS IN YOU, SWEETHEART, AND IT'S BYE-BYE TAR-ZAN.
- THERE WAS SOMETHING ELSE.
- WHAT?
- A NUMBER: **UPS474**. MEAN ANYTHING?
- NO. BUT LET ME SEE WHAT I CAN FIND OUT ABOUT IT. CHECK BACK IN A FEW DAYS. IN THE MEANTIME STAY AWAY FROM THE **P-4** STUFF. ONE LAST THING, TARZAN.
- WHAT?
- DOING ANYTHING TONIGHT?
- YEAH, RENTING MYSELF A PLANE TO FLY ME TO IRON MOUNTAIN. WHY?
- GOT TIME FOR A COMPUTER DATE?
- SORRY, ZAN. GOTTA RUN. I'LL SEND YOU PAYMENT THE USUAL WAY.
- THANKS TARZAN. BYE.
- BYE, ZAN.

END OF COMPUTER CONVERSATION

Dakota King's
Microdiary Entry #3
Re: Operation Black Fang

I had to find out more about UPS474, so I used my connections with Z.O.O. Headquarters to get me inside Iron Mountain to talk to somebody.

In two days I had what I wanted, a Top Secret Clearance Pass (good for only five days—thanks a lot, Boss!) and an "official" F.B.I. badge that would at least get me inside for a quick look.

Iron Mountain was a good name for the place. It was a hive of small laboratory rooms carved into the middle of a gigantic hump of stone, a small mountain once mined for its iron ore. Now it was a fortress. Two soldiers guarded a gate which led to the mouth of what looked like a mammoth cave sealed by the biggest steel door I have ever seen in my life. I managed to sneak a quick shot with my belt-buckle camera. (Note: Boss, this photo didn't come out. Sorry.)

My phony papers got me straight through the first level of security. As an armed guard led me through a maze of hallways deep in the lab, I studied the layout of the place. I particularly noticed a door we passed that said: DANGER! NEUROTOXINS WITHIN. NO ONE ALLOWED IN WITHOUT SECURITY CLEARANCE.

An armed guard led me to the office of Dr. Viktor Herbert who, the sign on the door told me, was the head of the Toxin Research Facility. Herbert was a short, roly-poly sort of guy with thinning gray hair and a pair of gold-rimmed glasses that magnified his alert brown eyes. My eyes swept the room, taking in all I could as I was sitting down. In that instant I tried to apply what I had learned from the Game of the Stones. It was a game my Ninja master had taught me when I was seventeen.

"Everyone looks," the Master had explained to me quietly, "but few really see." And with that he had set before me a small box with an intricately carved lid. Inside, he explained, were several objects. When he opened the lid, I was to look inside and take as long as I wanted to study the contents. When I felt I had looked long enough, he would close the box and ask me to describe each object inside—its color, size, and location in the box. It sounded very simple.

Slowly the Master opened the lid. I looked in and saw many red, black, and green gems, some silver coins, and one or two polished rocks. After I had stared at them for ten minutes, he asked me to tell him how many gems, stones, and coins were inside. To my surprise, I could barely remember half the contents of the box. But after more and more practice I was eventually able to glance into the box for less than five seconds and see all. For my final test, the Ninja master had opened a box, the bottom of which was covered with silver coins. All were identical except for the date. I was able to remember the exact date of each coin. Ever since then I have been able to look and really see.

Sometimes, however, my memory needs a rest. So I clicked on my belt-buckle camera. And just as I did, Dr. Herbert approached and stood right in front of me. Later I found out that my belt buckle took a picture of his belt buckle!

Luckily my memory didn't sleep too soundly, and I

took in every detail that might prove important later on. My Oriental way of seeing helped me zero in on the few things that might tell me more about Herbert. Like the **dusty photo of him in an army uniform with some other men.**

He caught me looking at it. "Me and my old army buddies," he explained. "We were all in the same unit in World War Two." I studied the photo, which showed Herbert, then a much younger man, wearing a **uniform with pilot's wings.**

Later, I drew the attached sketch of the photo from memory:

CLUE #4

After studying the picture, I quickly scanned the rest of the neat, orderly room. There were the usual family pictures and—not so usual—Indian artifacts, one of which was a **rare Indian doll.**

CLUE #5

I studied the rest of Dr. Herbert's office. Not much else unusual except for a **portable painted green metal oxygen tank** and mask in the corner. Herbert ushered me to a chair. Leaning heavily on a cane as he moved, he told me he had **sprained his ankle on a hike** he had taken earlier that week. He eased himself into a chair behind the metal desk. He laid the cane aside, lifted up the pipe from his desk, and stuck it into his mouth. With his **left hand** he struck a match from the **book of matches** on his desk, and took a few puffs.

I pressed the button on my watch and recorded the following:

****

TRANSCRIPT

VH: NOW, MR. KING, TELL ME WHAT I CAN DO FOR YOU AND THE F.B.I.

DK: TO COME RIGHT TO THE POINT, MY OFFICE HAS GOTTEN A REPORT THAT THERE HAVE BEEN CERTAIN AMOUNTS OF DANGEROUS MATERIALS LEAKING OUT OF YOUR LABORATORY.

VH: I DON'T KNOW WHAT YOUR PEOPLE TOLD YOU. . . OH, MAY I SEE YOUR IDENTIFICATION, PLEASE? JUST ROUTINE, YOU UNDERSTAND. HMMM, IT'S GOING TO EXPIRE IN A FEW DAYS. YOU BETTER GET IT RENEWED.

ANYWAY, AS YOU PROBABLY ALREADY KNOW, WHAT WE ARE DOING HERE IS TRYING TO DESIGN DISEASES FOR THE MILITARY. WE THINK THAT FUTURE WARS AREN'T GOING TO BE FOUGHT WITH GUNS BUT WITH GERMS. THINK OF IT. YOU PICK OUT A CUSTOM-MADE GERM, AS IT IS SOMETIMES CALLED, MIX SOME OF THESE POWERFUL GERMS UP IN A BATCH OF WATER, LOAD IT ONTO A PLANE, AND SPRAY IT AT ENEMY TROOPS. IN A FEW DAYS THEY'LL BE SO SICK, THEY'LL BE HAPPY TO SURRENDER.

WHAT WE DO IS TAKE APART THE MOLECULES AND VIRUSES THAT MAKE A DISEASE WORK, THROW OUT ALL THE PARTS THAT DON'T MATTER, AND PUT THE

MOLECULES AND VIRUSES BACK TOGETHER AGAIN SO WE HAVE A STREAMLINED GERM. IT'S COMPLICATED, BUT EFFECTIVE.

DK: YOU MEAN YOU TAKE A DISEASE AND MAKE IT EVEN DEADLIER?

VH: THAT'S ONE WAY OF PUTTING IT. WE LIKE TO THINK OF IT AS IMPROVING ON MOTHER NATURE. YOU KNOW, WE HAVE A BATCH OF BLACK WIDOW. . . WELL, IN A NUTSHELL, THAT'S WHAT WE DO.

DK: GETTING BACK TO MY FIRST QUESTION, HAVE YOU EVER LOST ANY OF YOUR POISONS?

VH: NEVER, MR. KING! ANY OF OUR POISONS IN THE HANDS OF AN ENEMY COUNTRY OR EVEN A POWER-HUNGRY INDIVIDUAL COULD BE DISASTROUS FOR THE WORLD. THE SERUM WOULD MAKE ANYONE WHO STOLE IT AND SOLD IT TO FOREIGN ENEMIES RICH. THERE ISN'T A FLY THAT GETS OUT OF HERE UNLESS IT HAS THE RIGHT CLEARANCE PAPERS. OUR LABS ARE SEALED UP SO TIGHT EVEN THE AIR INSIDE IS CLASSIFIED. WHEN WE'RE THROUGH HERE, I'LL SHOW YOU HOW GOOD OUR PROTECTION IS.

DK: BEFORE WE GO, DR. HERBERT, I HAVE ONE MORE SPECIFIC QUESTION. COULD YOU CHECK AND SEE IF YOU CAN ACCOUNT FOR YOUR FULL STOCK OF UPS474? [HIS PIPE ALMOST FELL OUT OF HIS MOUTH WHEN HE HEARD THIS.]

VH: I'M SORRY, MR. KING, I CANNOT DISCUSS ANY PARTICULAR PROJECT WITH YOU UNTIL YOU GET A HIGHER-LEVEL CLEARANCE. NOW, WOULD YOU LIKE TO LOOK AT OUR LABS OR NOT?

END OF TRANSCRIPT

****

Dakota King's
Microdiary Entry #4
Re: Operation Black Fang

Up until I had mentioned UPS474, Dr. Herbert had seemed friendly, almost jolly. When that number came up, he froze. I could tell I had hit a nerve, but then he recovered quickly. He grabbed the portable oxygen tank and his cane, and we began the tour.

The first laboratory he showed me was impressive. In some sections the technicians wore what looked like space suits with helmets and little air tanks on their backs. They carried the poisons around in small, flat, numbered bottles. In another section some researchers were handling the poison bottles through a glass box. Special armholes with long gloves built right into them let someone standing outside the box handle the material inside.

Herbert stood back as I scanned the layout. I clicked on my recorder:

****

TRANSCRIPT

VH: IMPRESSIVE PLACE, ISN'T IT?

DK: SURE IS. HOW DO YOU KEEP IT ALL SECURE?

VH: Look up at the ceilings, please. You will notice there is a camera up near each corner of the room. Each is connected to a TV screen watched by a separate guard. **No one could get anything out of here without its being noticed.** And even if they did, they would have to go past one guard after another. [He stopped to rest before going on. He took a whiff of oxygen from his portable tank.] Excuse me, I have a bad breathing problem. It's going to force me into early retirement, probably by the end of this year. Come this way, please. [Out the door and into the hallway.] Down this corridor are the other laboratories. Notice that each door has a special airlock everyone must go through on entering or leaving the room. Special electronic sensors at each exit door detect any leaks or molecules stuck to a person's clothing. It's all a very snug operation.

Now should anything or anyone start to escape, all kinds of things happen. Every door to every lab is automatically locked by the master computer. Extra security cameras like that one [he pointed to a camera up near the ceiling] are turned on. And under each tile on this floor is a special weight sensor. Once we click on the sensor system we can tell where everybody is by looking at control panels in our central office. [We continued walking. On our way back to his office, a woman, much younger than Herbert, stopped us. Herbert seemed to know her.] Ah! Lucy. I'd like you to meet a visitor. Lucy Dorman, this is Dakota King.

LD: Lucille Dorman to you, Viktor. [She turned to me.] Dakota? Your parents named you after a state? Isn't that a little strange? [She shook

MY HAND WITH A STRONG GRIP. **OBVIOUSLY A WOMAN WHO LIKED PHYSICAL ACTIVITIES. SHE HAD THE TAN OF SOMEONE WHO SPENT A LOT OF TIME OUT-OF-DOORS.**]

DK: NOT REALLY. IT WAS MY PARENTS' FAVORITE STATE.

LD: WHICH ONE, NORTH OR SOUTH?

DK: ACTUALLY, BOTH. MY MOTHER WAS FROM NORTH DAKOTA, MY FATHER FROM SOUTH DAKOTA, AND. . .

LD: [CUTTING ME OFF.] INTERESTING. AH, HERBERT, I HAVE A BONE TO PICK WITH YOU. SOME OF THOSE BLOCKHEADS IN MEDICAL SUPPLIES DELIVERED MORE OF YOUR OXYGEN TANKS TO MY OFFICE BY MISTAKE. I CAN BARELY TURN AROUND BECAUSE OF ALL THE TANKS IN MY OFFICE. I WISH YOU'D GET THE DIRECTIONS STRAIGHT WITH THEM.

VH: NOW WAIT A MINUTE, LUCY. . .

LD: AND ANOTHER THING. FOR SOME REASON THE SWITCHBOARD SENT SOME OF YOUR CALLS THROUGH TO MY PHONE. I TOOK THIS ONE MESSAGE DOWN BECAUSE IT SEEMED IMPORTANT, BUT THIS IS THE LAST TIME I PLAY SECRETARY FOR YOU. [SHE HANDED HIM A PIECE OF PAPER.] YOU MAY NOT TAKE ME SERIOUSLY AS A SCIENTIST, BUT EVERYONE ELSE AROUND HERE DOES. GOOD DAY. NICE MEETING YOU, MR. NEVADA SMITH. [SHE WALKED AWAY.]

DK: AH, THAT'S <u>DAKOTA</u>, MA'AM. . . .

END OF TRANSCRIPT

****

Dr. Herbert seemed relieved to see Ms. Dorman go. As we moved down the hall toward his office, he read the phone message she gave him. I couldn't help but notice—all right, I snooped—that it was notepaper with strange markings on it. But there was something else about it that seemed familiar. I put my belt buckle to work again and snapped this picture:

CLUE #6

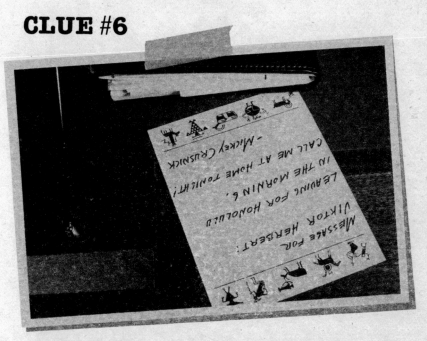

After he glanced over the note, Herbert talked about the other security measures used in Iron Mountain Lab: specially trained attack dogs, specially trained sentries, and—best of all—the fact that there was only one way out.

With the whole lab complex built into a mountain, it was much easier to keep an eye on where everything went. When we returned to Herbert's office, he sat down and sketched out the area where the labs were. He drew it as a large hump of rock with nothing but open land for hundreds of miles in every direction. The place was leakproof, Boss. How anybody or anything could get out of there without being caught is beyond me. But someone did.

From the desk of **Dr. Viktor Herbert**

Dakota King's
Microdiary Entry #5
Re: Operation Black Fang

    I thanked Herbert for his help and headed toward the front gate. On my way out a tall, sandy-haired man wearing coveralls went rushing past me. He was moving so fast he almost knocked me down. I turned to tell him to watch where he was going when I noticed that he was carrying a white styrofoam cooler, the kind of thing you take on a picnic or a trip to the beach. What caught my attention was a wide band of masking tape stuck to its side. Someone had written across it: UPS474. I turned and followed him at a distance.

    One corridor turned into another and another as he walked for what seemed to be miles. Finally, as he turned one corner, I had to stop short and back away— just in the nick of time. He had paused to talk to Dr. Herbert! I turned on my wristwatch recorder:

****

TRANSCRIPT

VH: YOU! WHAT ARE YOU DOING HERE?

MAN: [MUMBLING. COULDN'T MAKE OUT ANSWER.]

VH: THIS BETTER BE YOUR LAST VISIT. WHAT IS THIS FOR?

MAN: [STILL MUMBLING.]. . . 74.

VH: WHO ORDERED THIS? I DIDN'T.

MAN: [MORE MUMBLING.]

VH: OH SHE DID, DID SHE?

MAN: [MORE MUMBLING.]

VH: WHAT? DON'T WORRY. DON'T WORRY. YOU'LL GET IT. I'LL SEND YOU THE. . . [JUST THEN A GUARD CAME WALKING BY. HERBERT STOPPED TALKING AND QUICKLY DISAPPEARED DOWN A SIDE CORRIDOR. THE MAN CONTINUED ON. I FOLLOWED BEHIND UNTIL HE PAUSED BEFORE A DOOR MARKED SPECIMEN HOLDING AREA. TO ONE SIDE WAS A SMALL SPEAKER AND A BUTTON. HE PUSHED THE BUTTON, AND A VOICE CAME ON.]

VOICE: STEP BACK ONTO THE WHITE SQUARE, PLEASE, AND IDENTIFY YOUR MISSION.

MAN: DELIVERY.

VOICE: PROJECT NUMBER?

MAN: UPS474. [A BUZZER SOUNDED, AND THE MAN STEPPED INSIDE. THEN, A MINUTE OR SO LATER, HE CAME OUT AGAIN. OFF TO MY RIGHT WAS AN UNMARKED DOOR. I TOOK A CHANCE AND JUMPED INSIDE TO AVOID BEING SEEN. LUCK WAS WITH ME—IT WAS A SUPPLY CLOSET, AND I FOUND A LAB ASSISTANT'S WHITE COVERALLS HANGING ON A HOOK. I PUT THEM ON AND PEEKED OUT INTO THE CORRIDOR—IT WAS EMPTY. SO I SAUNTERED NONCHALANTLY BUT PURPOSE-FULLY UP TO THE SPECIMEN HOLDING AREA AND PRESSED THE BUTTON. AGAIN THE VOICE ANSWERED OVER THE SPEAKER.]

VOICE: YOUR MISSION?

DK: I'M MAKING A PICKUP.

VOICE: Project number?

DK: UPS474. [The buzzer sounded, and I stepped inside a small room with a caged window in it. Behind it stood a bored-looking guard.]

GUARD: Why don't you people get organized? This just got here. [He went to the back and brought out the cooler the man had brought in. He slid a clipboard with a form on it under my nose.] Sign here. [I signed your name on the list—sorry, boss.]

END OF TRANSCRIPT

****

I took the cooler and slipped back into the supply closet where I had found the coveralls, turned on an overhead light, and closed the door. Inside the cooler were two large plastic bags misted over with condensation. Very strange. Pressing my face against one, I looked in. When some of the mist cleared away, I saw a slitted eye staring straight back at me. I jerked back for a second, then looked again. I saw a pair of eyes. And there were at least four or five other pairs of eyes in there. Slipping a small knife from my ankle sheath, I cut open the bag and dumped its contents on the floor. The heads of four cobras, huge snakes judging by the heads, came tumbling out. I picked one up to take a closer look. It had long fangs. It was frozen solid, its mouth opened in a permanent state of attack.

Just then I heard a noise behind me, but before I had time to react I felt **a blow on the back of my neck.** My eyes saw rosy rings of light that got smaller and smaller until they receded into total darkness.

When I awoke, the cooler was gone, the snake heads

were gone, and the back of my neck was sore and aching. As my eyes began to pull into focus again, I noticed that there was one head left. But as I looked more closely I saw it was attached to a long, long body. It was very, very much alive and interested—in me!

For some reason it hadn't attacked while I was unconscious, maybe because I was lying so still. But as soon as I stirred, it slithered backward and gathered its immense length into one big coil for attack. Keeping as still as possible, I glanced carefully around the small closet. There were some dusty boxes, an old raincoat, an umbrella, a broom, a couple of mops, and a pail. In that one glance I could see I had a serious problem. This snake was too big to kill—even if I still had my knife. There was no way to make a safe exit. The snake was coiled between me and the door. If I could somehow move the snake to one side, I might be able to reach the door and get out.

From my boyhood days of watching snake charmers entertaining the tourists near the gate of the old city in Fez, Morocco, I remembered that the power of the snake charmer was not his music, but in the swaying he did as he played his flute. Hoping this snake went to the same charm school, I inched my sweating hand over to one of the mops that was just within reach and slowly pushed it toward the serpent. It hissed and reared but was obviously confused.

It backed up, too, but not enough. I kept swaying the mop back and forth. The cobra followed the same rhythm, but it didn't move an inch. I remember wondering if we were going to dance like that all day. Rummaging quietly around in my pockets, I found the small plastic cigarette lighter I had hidden from Longh Gonh during our training hike. (I never was able to build a fire as fast as he, so when his back was turned, I would click on the lighter and start the fire. He never learned how I did it.)

The mop I was holding was bone dry, so I clicked on the lighter and lit the mop head. The flames caught. The snake began to slither backwards—not as fast as I hoped, but at least it was moving. I lunged forward with the fiery mop, and it reared backwards another inch or so. This went on for about ten seconds when I saw that my mop was burning up faster than I thought. Time was running out. The snake still wasn't moving away fast enough. I had to get to that doorknob. I reached for it, but the snake lunged forward in spite of the flames, which were now quite low.

I jumped back, holding the smoldering mop between me and it. Then I thrust the mop straight at the cobra's head. Only then did it slither backwards. But it coiled up, its hood flared, ready for another strike. In the meantime the mop had burned out. I could think of nothing else to do but sway the charred handle back and forth to keep the critter busy. I was backed up against the wall, choking from the smoke and looking for another weapon, when I felt the handle of the umbrella behind me. I looked down at the handle and saw it was one of those fast-opening, push-button types. It was my last chance, and I had to take it.

Holding the charred mop in my left hand and the umbrella in my right, I slid toward the door. The snake did not move. The next second I lunged. Swinging sideways, I hit the side of the snake's neck with the mop handle. It hissed and swayed backwards. A split second later I jumped at the door. My hand had barely touched the doorknob when the snake hurled its fanged head at me. I held the umbrella up in front of me and pressed the button. The black umbrella popped open, leaving a fragile shell of nylon between me and the snake. Its fangs popped through the black fabric but missed me.

With my free hand I twisted the knob, and the door swung open. I pushed the umbrella and the slithering body of the snake back inside and slammed the door. I could hear the serpent banging around in there with the umbrella. After wiping the sweat off my face and straightening out my clothes, I left Iron Mountain Laboratory, fast.

GET A LOAD OF THIS HISSER, BOSS!

Dakota King's
Microdiary Entry #6
Re: <u>Operation Black Fang</u>

After my encounter with the snake, I was more convinced than ever that whatever UPS474 was, it had to be important enough to make someone try to get rid of the F.B.I. agent I was pretending to be. I <u>had</u> to find out what UPS474 was! The back of my neck still throbbed with the memory of the bump I'd gotten in the closet, but Longh Gonh showed me no sympathy. "You must learn to withstand the little pains, Dakota," he said, "so that you may better withstand the greater ones." Sure. Easy for him to say. I was the one with the lump the size of a walnut at the base of my skull! Despite my minor complaints, the next morning Longh and I were back on the road to Iron Mountain.

Ten miles from the entrance to the lab, a billboard caught my eye. "Visit Jungle Ed's Snake Farm and Alligator Wrestling Emporium." Right up there, ten feet tall, dressed like a white hunter in safari clothes, was Jungle Ed. It looked like the guy I'd seen carrying that cooler full of snake heads! Instantly, Ed became our next suspect. No use going any farther until we checked him out first. So Longh and I headed back to my small lab at the Disappearing, Inc. office.

The first thing I did was call up the Emporium to find out what Jungle Ed's last name was. Then it was a simple matter of clicking on my computer and asking Zan what she could get for me. I typed in the following:

```
O    O        COMPUTER CONVERSATION        O    O
O    O                                     O    O
O                                               O
O    ATTENTION: ZAN                             O
O    SUBJECT: INFORMATION ON ONE JUNGLE ED      O
O    RYAN, SNAKE AND ALLIGATOR EMPORIUM         O
O    OWNER, BARE RANCH, DEATH VALLEY.           O
O    NEED: AS SOON AS POSSIBLE. DOUBLE PAY-     O
O    MENT FOR SERVICE.                          O
O                                               O
O         END OF COMPUTER CONVERSATION          O
O                                               O
```

Dakota King's
Microdiary Entry #7
Re: Operation Black Fang

    The next morning, with a snakebite kit in the glove compartment of our car, Longh and I headed out to see Jungle Ed. We found him napping in his trailer office. He was a tall blond man wearing a dirty safari suit. A sweat-stained hat with a leopardskin headband was tilted down over his eyes. Curled up on his chest was a baby boa constrictor. I clicked on my wrist recorder, stepped inside, and taped this conversation:

****

TRANSCRIPT

DK: [WHISPERING—HARD TO HEAR.] JUNGLE ED. JUNGLE ED, WAKE UP. THERE'S A SNAKE ON YOU.

JE: [WHISPERING.] I KNOW. DON'T DISTURB HIM. HE'S HAD A TOUGH NIGHT. HE JUST FLEW IN FROM SOUTH AMERICA. WHAT CAN I DO FOR YOU?

DK: MY NAME IS KING, DAKOTA KING. I'M CARRYING OUT AN INVESTIGATION FOR THE GOVERNMENT ABOUT SOME MISSING PROPERTY. . .

JE: HOLD ON, HERE! JUNGLE ED NEVER STOLE ANYTHING. [HE PUSHED HIS HAT UP. I RECOGNIZED HIM IMMEDIATELY. HE <u>WAS</u> THE MAN WITH THE COOLER. THE

MAN I SAW TALKING TO HERBERT.] WHAT IS IT YOU SAY I TOOK?

DK: IT'S NOTHING WE THINK YOU TOOK. BUT SOMETHING IS MISSING, AND I'M JUST CHECKING TO SEE IF YOU KNOW ANYTHING ABOUT IT. SOMETHING CALLED UPS474.

JE: YOU MEAN THE **SNAKE STUFF**?

DK: YEAH, THE SNAKE STUFF. NOW, WHAT DID YOU HAVE TO DO WITH IT?

JE: ALL I KNOW IS I HAD AN AGREEMENT TO PROVIDE THE LAB WITH AS MANY SNAKES AS POSSIBLE.

DK: WHAT KIND OF SNAKES?

JE: **KING COBRAS**, MOSTLY. THEY'RE BIG SNAKES. POWERFUL VENOM. REAL KILLERS. ONE BITE FROM ONE OF THOSE, AND IN ABOUT THIRTY MINUTES IT'S BEDTIME FOR BONZO.

DK: DO YOU HAVE ANY HERE THAT I COULD SEE?

JE: SAY NO MORE. (HE GENTLY PICKED UP THE SLEEPING SNAKE AND SET IT ON THE DESK.) JUNGLE ED WILL SHOW YOU. (SOUNDS OF WALKING FOR YARDS AND YARDS. FOOTSTEPS STOP.) THERE'S ONE RIGHT HERE.

DK: IT LOOKS FAMILIAR.

LG: AND BIG.

JE: YOU A SNAKE EXPERT OR SOMETHING? YOU CAN GO IN AND HANDLE IT IF YOU'VE A MIND TO.

DK: NO THANKS. I'VE ALREADY HAD A GOOD LOOK AT ONE. HAVE YOU ALWAYS SUPPLIED THE LAB WITH KING COBRAS?

JE: YEAH, OFF AND ON. LATELY IT'S BEEN MOSTLY OFF. BUT TWO DAYS AGO I GOT A PANICKY CALL FROM THE LAB. THEY SAID THERE HAD BEEN AN ACCIDENT, AND ONE OF THEIR BATCHES WAS DESTROYED. COULD I RUSH OVER A DOZEN

SNAKES? WELL, THESE CRITTERS ARE HARD TO FIND. YOU CAN'T JUST DIAL-A-SNAKE AND GET ONE DELIVERED TO YOUR DOOR LIKE A PIZZA.

DK: SO DID YOU GET THE SNAKES?

JE: NOT EXACTLY, BUT I GOT THE NEXT BEST THING. SINCE ALL THE LAB PEOPLE WANT IS THE POISON, I TRACKED DOWN A BUNCH OF LOCAL SNAKE HANDLERS WHO HAD SOME OLD COBRAS. I PAID THEM A GOOD CASH PRICE FOR THEIR HEADS—THAT'S WHERE ALL THE POISON IS CONCENTRATED—AND DELIVERED THEM TO THE LAB. I'M NOT EXACTLY SURE WHAT THEY DO WITH THE SNAKES, BUT FROM WHAT I'VE HEARD—NOW THIS IS ONLY RUMORS, YOU UNDERSTAND—THEY EXTRACT THE POISON AND DO SOMETHING WITH IT. ALL I KNOW IS THAT THEY GIVE ME THIS CODE NUMBER FOR WHEN I DELIVER THE STUFF.

DK: WHO IS IT FOR?

JE: SOMEONE IN HERBERT'S LABORATORY.

LG: WAS HE THE ONE WHO CALLED YOU?

JE: NO, IT WAS A SHE. LUCILLE SOMEBODY.

LG: DID YOU DELIVER THE SNAKE HEADS TO HER?

JE: NOPE. DROPPED THEM OFF AT THE MAIN DELIVERY ROOM AS USUAL. HEY, YOU WANT TO TAKE A PERSONALLY GUIDED TOUR AROUND MY SNAKE FARM? I CAN SHOW IT TO YOU BEFORE THE TOURISTS COME RUSHING IN.

DK: ER, NO THANKS, JUNGLE ED. CATCH YOU LATER. LONGH AND I HAVE TO GET GOING.

END OF TRANSCRIPT

****

Dakota King's
Microdiary Entry #8
Re: Operation Black Fang

As we walked back to the car, Longh asked without looking at me, "Well, Dakota, what do you think about Mr. Jungle Ed? Could he be the thief who walked off with the poison?"

"Don't know. Let's see what the computer finds. I do know one thing. Jungle Ed is definitely the same guy I saw with Herbert."

"He is? Hmmmm," said Longh. "Consider this possibility. Perhaps he saw you following him and doubled back once you were hidden in the broom closet."

"Could be. The thing is I didn't see anyone open the door before I got bopped on the head," I said. "Either someone was in there waiting, or they managed to get in some other way."

"What other way?" Longh asked. "How many doors were there to that room?"

"Just one. But no one came in by the door. I'm sure of it," I answered. "But I'm also sure Ed does a lot more than just show snakes to odd tourists suckered into visiting his pathetic snake farm. He seemed awful eager to get us out of his office."

"Yes, I observed that, too," agreed Longh. "Perhaps we can figure out something from the photographs."

"Uh . . . what photographs?" I wanted to know.

"En route to Jungle Ed's office, I photographed the rest of the trailer. Did you not notice I was wearing your belt-buckle camera, Dakota? When we return to the office, we can develop the photographs."

CLUE #7

That night Longh took his roll of fast-developing film and put it into a special quick-processing gizmo I invented. In about ten minutes we had a series of pictures of Ed's layout. Jungle Ed's office was at one end of the trailer, and at the other end were two rooms, both empty. His living quarters appeared to be a bedroom with a few clothes strewn about and a tiny kitchen with the remains of a meal and some dirty dishes in the sink. As a group, the pictures aroused my curiousity, especially one blurred photo of a half-opened closet where there was a suitcase with an envelope on top. I couldn't make out the papers sticking out of the envelope, so I put the film under my super-enlarger that can blow up an ant to the size of Godzilla! Those papers sticking out of the envelope were plane tickets! To where we couldn't tell, since the destination was on the reverse side.

While Longh and I studied the photos, my phone rang. I let my answering machine get it, but I listened to see who it was. All the voice said was: "This is Zan. You got it. You'll find it in the network in your code name." I ran to my computer and typed in my secret code. In a flash, there was her report:

COMPUTER REPORT

__SUBJECT:__ JUNGLE ED RYAN, ALIAS EDWARD DE BRACK, ALIAS **MICKEY CRUSNICK**

__PRESENT OCCUPATION:__ SNAKE OWNER & ENTERTAINER

__PAST OCCUPATIONS:__ CAR MECHANIC, WAITER,

SNAKE HANDLER IN ZOO, ROOF REPAIRMAN, DOOR-TO-DOOR SALESMAN, BARTENDER, AND **EX-CONVICT**

RECORD OF ARRESTS: 1976—EXTORTION: SERVED 2 YEARS IN PRISON 1979—WRITING BAD CHECKS: SERVED THREE YEARS

PERSONAL DETAILS: LIVES ALONE WITH HIS COCKER SPANIEL, FANG, AND IS KNOWN TO BE A COMPULSIVE GAMBLER. A CHECK OF HIS BANK RECORDS SHOWS THAT JUNGLE ED'S SNAKE EMPORIUM IS GOING TO THE DOGS. HE HAD TO **SELL OFF HIS OWN AIRPLANE** TO KEEP BUSINESS AFLOAT. PEOPLE AREN'T THAT INTERESTED IN SNAKES AND ALLIGATORS ANY-MORE. **EMPORIUM MIGHT BE GOING OUT OF BUSI-NESS UNLESS HE GETS SOME MONEY SOON.** NO CURRENT ARREST RECORD. HE SEEMS TO HAVE KEPT HIS NOSE CLEAN IN RECENT YEARS. THIS IS ALL I COULD FIND OUT ON SUCH SHORT NOTICE.

LOVE AND XXXX'S

—ZAN

END OF REPORT

Dakota King's
Microdiary Entry #9
Re: Operation Black Fang

"It all makes perfect sense," said Longh, reading Zan's report. "Our Mr. Jungle Ed was clearly in need of money and, as his record shows, honesty was never his best policy. He could have hijacked UPS474 and sold it to the highest bidder. There would be many who might want the germ serum. One who had it would have the power to control the world," Longh logically concluded.

"True," I said. "But somehow I feel that almost all of what he told me was the truth. Ed is a small-time crook. He doesn't have enough skill to try and defeat the security system of Iron Mountain. Someone on the inside would have less of a problem. Someone like Lucille Dorman. An insider would be more likely to know what foreign agents to contact about selling the serum. Before we check out Jungle Ed any further, I want to find out what Ms. Dorman is all about."

I called the laboratory to see if she was there. It was her day off, I was told. And she was spending it the way she usually did, **rock climbing,** on one of the tall stone pillars out on the edge of the Indian reservation.

"I'm going out, Longh," I announced.

"Where?"

"To do some mountain climbing," I shouted over my shoulder as I whizzed out the door. "While I'm gone, see what you can find out about Viktor Herbert, too. I'll be back later, and we can compare notes.

"Dakota! Mountain climbing? For your sake, let us hope Ms. Dorman is a beginner," Longh said drily. Sometimes he forgets who signs his paycheck!

I jumped into my jeep and headed out toward the climbers' rocks. After a couple of hours of scanning the area with my binoculars, I spotted this tiny flyspeck of a person scampering down the side of a cliff. I parked the jeep and waited for Lucille Dorman to come down. Eventually she saw me and came strolling over, barely winded from her strenuous climb. Lucille Dorman had a small but strong-looking body, short brown hair, and pale gray eyes that seemed to look through you. She acted more annoyed than surprised to see me. As she approached I clicked on my wrist recorder:

****

TRANSCRIPT

DK: MS. DORMAN! I THOUGHT I RECOGNIZED YOU. I DON'T KNOW IF YOU REMEMBER ME. . . .

LD: OH YES, YOU'RE THE ONE WHO WAS WITH VIKTOR YESTERDAY. YOU'RE NAMED AFTER A STATE.

DK: THAT'S RIGHT. DAKOTA. . .

LD: WELL, WELL. IT WAS NICE TO SEE YOU AGAIN. NOW IF YOU'LL EXCUSE ME, I'VE GOT TO GO.

DK: HEY, WAIT A MINUTE. CAN I GIVE YOU A RIDE?

LD: NO, THANKS. I LIKE WALKING. [SOUNDS OF FEET SCRAMBLING ON ROCKS.]

DK: IT'S GOING TO BE A LONG, HOT WALK. [I PUT THE JEEP IN GEAR AND SLOWLY

DROVE ALONGSIDE HER.] THE SUN'S GETTING HIGHER. SURE YOU DON'T WANT TO
RECONSIDER?

LD: [NO ANSWER.]

DK: I'VE GOT COOL KOOL-AID.

LD: [NO ANSWER.]

DK: AND GATORADE.

LD: ALL RIGHT. ALL RIGHT. I'LL TAKE THE RIDE. WHERE'S THE GATORADE?

DK: RIGHT HERE. YOU MUST GET AWFUL THIRSTY OUT THERE ON THE ROCKS.

LD: A BIT. BUT I TRY TO GET STARTED SHORTLY AFTER DAWN WHEN IT'S A
LITTLE COOLER. EVEN SO, WHAT WATER I CARRY GOES PRETTY QUICKLY. I HAVE TO
BE CAREFUL ABOUT CONSERVING IT. THIS IS USUALLY ALL I NEED. [SHE HELD UP
AN OLD BEAT-UP CANTEEN. IT WAS BANGED UP SO MUCH THAT **MUCH OF THE
GREEN PAINT COVERING IT HAD BEEN SCRAPED OFF.**]

DK: YOU DO A LOT OF ROCK CLIMBING? I MEAN, IT SEEMS LIKE A KIND OF
ROUGH SPORT FOR A WOMAN.

LD: NOT AT ALL, MR. KING. IT IS ONE OF THE MANY THINGS THAT WOMEN CAN
DO BETTER THAN MEN. [SHE GLARED AT ME.] BESIDES, I FIND IT AN EXCELLENT
WAY TO RELAX AND CLEAR MY HEAD.

DK: TO RELAX! ALL I CAN THINK OF WHEN I'M UP HIGH IS HOW FAR I CAN FALL.

LD: WELL, I GUESS THAT'S YOUR PROBLEM.

DK: [TIME TO CHANGE THE SUBJECT.] WHAT DO YOU NEED TO CLEAR YOUR
HEAD FOR? YOU HAVE SOME PROBLEMS AT THE LAB?

LD: IT HAS NOTHING TO DO WITH THE LAB. I'M DUE TO COMPETE IN A KARATE
COMPETITION TOMORROW. GOING OUT FOR A GOOD CLIMB LETS ME THINK
THROUGH MY FIGHT STRATEGIES.

DK: Wonderful sport, karate. You just starting?

LD: Hardly. I have a black belt, Mr. Dakota.

DK: It's King. Dakota King. Oh, well. I guess I'm surprised. Somehow I didn't think of you as being so athletic. I guess it's because you're so, uhm. . .short.

LD: We can't all be towering giants like you, Mr. King, now can we? We just have to try and make do with what we have. I've always been quite athletic.

DK: Okay. Sorry, I just meant you must keep pretty active. Are you from this part of the country, Ms. Dorman?

LD: If you mean this part of the West, no. I was born and raised in Oregon and took up rock climbing in Yosemite Park while I was going to college. And what brings you out to the desert this morning? Not rock climbing, too?

DK: Er. . .no. I've been fossil hunting.

LD: Oh, really? And what kinds of fossils?

DK: Ahhh. . .uhm. Prehistoric snails.

LD: That's odd. I do a little fossil hunting myself, and I've never heard of snail fossils having been discovered in this region. How many did you find?

DK: None yet. I guess that explains why.

LD: Any OTHER reason why you just happened to be driving by?

DK: Okay. I'll tell you the truth. I wasn't fossil hunting.

LD: My, my, am I surprised!

DK: Look. There are some strange things going on in your lab, and

I'VE BEEN GIVEN THE JOB BY THE F.B.I. TO FIND OUT WHO'S BEHIND THEM.

LD: STRANGE THINGS? SUCH AS?

DK: SUCH AS THE RUMORS THAT SOME OF YOUR TOP SECRET POISONS HAVE BEEN STOLEN. MAYBE. . . UPS474?

LD: [SURPRISED.] WHAT <u>ABOUT</u> UPS474?

DK: WHY DON'T YOU TELL ME?

LD: I HAVE A BETTER IDEA. WHY DON'T <u>YOU</u> TELL <u>ME</u> WHAT AUTHORITY YOU HAVE TO ASK THESE QUESTIONS?

DK: I THINK THIS SHOULD SATISFY YOU. [TAKING ONE HAND OFF THE STEERING WHEEL, I REACHED INTO MY POCKET, PULLED OUT ONE OF MY MANY FAKE IDENTITY CARDS, AND HANDED IT TO HER. SHE TOOK IT AND LOOKED AT IT WITH AN ASTONISHED EXPRESSION.]

LD: WHY SHOULD A LIBRARY CARD FROM BISMARCK, NORTH DAKOTA, GIVE YOU ANY AUTHORITY?

DK: WHAT! OOPS, WRONG CARD. HERE.

LD: F.B.I. HMMM. WHAT IS IT YOU NEED TO KNOW EXACTLY?

DK: FIRST, TELL ME A LITTLE ABOUT WHAT YOU DO AT IRON MOUNTAIN.

LD: TO PUT IT BLUNTLY, I DO ALL THE WORK HERBERT IS SUPPOSED TO DO. YOU SEE, I WAS ONE OF HIS STUDENTS WHEN HE TAUGHT AT COLLEGE, AND LATER HE HIRED ME ON AT THE LABORATORY.

DK: DON'T YOU MIND HIS GETTING ALL THE CREDIT?

LD: OF COURSE. BUT HE IS GOING TO LEAVE SOON, AND I EXPECT TO GET HIS JOB. THEN, FINALLY, I'LL GET THE CREDIT. HE MAY HAVE TO RETIRE SOONER THAN HE PLANNED. THIS MYSTERIOUS **BREATHING PROBLEM** HAS REALLY SLOWED HIM DOWN. IT'S SO STRANGE. HE SEEMED SO HEALTHY ONE DAY, AND THEN THE NEXT

HE WAS HANGING ON TO HIS OXYGEN TANK AS THOUGH IT WAS MADE OF GOLD. AND NOW HE HAS THIS **BAD LIMP**, TOO.

DK: I GUESS AS PEOPLE GET OLDER THEY GET MORE AILMENTS.

LD: MAYBE. I THINK THE PRESSURE OF HAVING TO WORK ON OPERATION BLACK FANG HAS BEEN TOO MUCH FOR HIM.

DK: [THIS WAS THE <u>FIRST</u> TIME I HEARD THE CODE NAME FOR THE PROJECT, BOSS. I ACTED AS THOUGH I KNEW WHAT SHE WAS TALKING ABOUT.] YOU MEAN UPS474.

LD: YES, OF COURSE. ESPECIALLY WITH THAT LATEST MYSTERIOUS LOSS OF MATERIAL. PEOPLE IN THE LAB ARE AMAZINGLY CARELESS, SO, FRANKLY, I'M NOT SURPRISED SOMETHING LIKE THAT HAPPENED.

DK: HERBERT TOLD ME EVERYTHING IS GUARDED LIKE THE GOLD AT FORT KNOX.

LD: THAT'S WHAT HE WOULD LIKE YOU TO BELIEVE. BUT THE FACT IS THERE WAS, AND IS, A LOT OF POISON MISSING.

DK: DO YOU KNOW A GUY NAMED JUNGLE ED?

LD: [A LITTLE NERVOUS.] UH . . . YES.

DK: HAD YOU CALLED HIM ON THE DAY I WAS THERE VISITING?

LD: YES. [SHE SEEMED REAL NERVOUS NOW.]

DK: WAS IT FOR SOME SORT OF EMERGENCY SHIPMENT?

LD: IS THAT AN OFFICIAL OR A FRIENDLY QUESTION?

DK: IT'S A FRIENDLY QUESTION, BUT IF YOU DON'T ANSWER IT I COULD TURN IT INTO AN OFFICIAL ONE.

LD: [FOR WHAT SEEMED LIKE MINUTES SHE SAID NOTHING. THEN SHE TOOK A DEEP BREATH.] ALL RIGHT, HERE'S WHAT HAPPENED. THERE WAS AN EMERGENCY NEED FOR SNAKES BECAUSE THERE WAS A **SUDDEN DISAPPEARANCE OF SOME**

UPS474 SUPERVENOM. AND IT WAS FROM MY DEPARTMENT. VIKTOR HERBERT DISCOVERED IT WAS GONE. HE SAID HE WAS GOING TO START AN INVESTIGATION IN TWENTY-FOUR HOURS UNLESS I WAS ABLE TO FIND IT. WELL, I COULDN'T FIND IT. SO I DECIDED TO DO THE NEXT BEST THING: MAKE MORE OF IT QUICKLY. ALL I HAD TO DO WAS TO BUY SOME MORE SNAKES FROM JUNGLE ED AND MAKE ANOTHER BATCH OF THE STUFF.

END OF TRANSCRIPT

****

At that moment we arrived in front of her house. She thanked me for the ride and hopped out.

I was getting a funny feeling about Ms. Lucille Dorman. I was thinking about her as I drove home. No love lost between her and Herbert. She could have stolen the poison to make Herbert and his department look bad. It could be one way of forcing him out of his job sooner.

I hurried home to see what Longh had found about Herbert. But when I got there, Longh Gonh was long gone. While I waited, I called Zan up on the computer to see what she could tell me about Lucille Dorman.

```
COMPUTER CONVERSATION

 • YOU RANG, MASTER?
 • YES ZAN. I'M LOOKING FOR INFORMATION
ABOUT A WOMAN.
 • IS SHE CUTE?
 • YEAH, I GUESS SO.
```

- CUTER THAN ME?
- OH I WOULDN'T GO THAT FAR. LET'S SAY SHE HAS A NICE PERSONALITY.
- WHAT DOES SHE DO?
- MAKES SNAKE POISON.
- WHAT KINDS OF GIRLS ARE YOU SEEING THESE DAYS, TARZAN? FORGET THE SNAKE WOMAN. GO FOR SOMEONE WITH SAFER HOBBIES. LIKE ME. OK, WHAT'S THIS SNAKE CHARMER'S NAME?
- LUCILLE DORMAN.
- WHERE IS SHE?
- WORKS AT IRON MOUNTAIN LABORATORIES. I'D LIKE TO KNOW MORE ABOUT HER AND SOMETHING CALLED OPERATION BLACK FANG.
- CUTE NAME. IT SOUNDS SIMPLE ENOUGH. IF YOU WANT TO HANG ON A SECOND, I MIGHT BE ABLE TO PULL SOMETHING OUT RIGHT NOW. WHY DON'T YOU HUM THE "BATTLE HYMN OF THE REPUBLIC" OR SOMETHING TO YOURSELF?
- OK.

END OF COMPUTER CONVERSATION

A minute or so later, my screen blinked into action.

COMPUTER REPORT

DORMAN WAS ONE OF HERBERT'S GRADU-
ATE STUDENTS IN COLLEGE. INTERESTINGLY,
SHE ALSO CLAIMED THAT <u>SHE</u> IS **THE ONE WHO
ORIGINALLY CAME UP WITH THE SPECIAL POISON-
MAKING METHOD THAT HERBERT HAS THE CREDIT
FOR.** SHE KICKED UP A PUBLIC FUSS, YET
LATER GOT A VERY GOOD JOB IN HERBERT'S
LAB. SHORTLY AFTER THAT SHE STOPPED COM-
PLAINING. SEEMS THEY BOUGHT HER OFF TO
KEEP HER QUIET.

ONE MORE INTERESTING ITEM. IT SEEMS
THAT IN ADDITION TO BEING A GOOD CLIMBER/
HIKER AND BLACK BELT, MS. DORMAN IS ALSO
A **TALENTED SKYDIVER.** SHE WAS IN THE LOCAL
PAPERS RECENTLY FOR HAVING MADE HER
1000TH JUMP. THOUGHT YOU'D LIKE TO
KNOW.

RE: OPERATION BLACK FANG
FOUND ONLY ONE SMALL REFERENCE IN AN
OBSCURE SCIENCE MAGAZINE. IT HAS SOME-
THING TO DO WITH MANUFACTURING SNAKE
VENOM IN A SPECIAL WAY. APPARENTLY GOOD

OLD DR. HERBERT (*OR* MS. DORMAN, IF SHE IS
TO BE BELIEVED) FIGURED OUT SOME METHOD
OF TAKING CHEMICALS APART AND PUTTING
THEM TOGETHER IN A NEW WAY THAT CAN
CHANGE THEM SOMEHOW. ACCORDING TO MY
SOURCES, OPERATION BLACK FANG INVOLVES
TAKING ORDINARY SNAKE VENOM AND MAKING
IT EVEN MORE POISONOUS BY CHANGING ITS
CHEMISTRY.

YOU KNOW WHERE TO SEND THE MONEY.
SAME PLACE. SAME TIME OF DAY. BYE NOW.
CHOCOLATES WOULD BE NICE TOO.

—ZAN

END OF REPORT

Dakota King's
Microdiary Entry #10
Re: Operation Black Fang

I headed back to Iron Mountain, but didn't get too far this time. Someone who was on to our little trick had contacted the F.B.I. They said they had never heard of me. Shortly after I got into the Iron Mountain complex, Herbert and a half dozen guards were at my heels. They escorted me to the front gate where Longh just happened to be waiting. Somehow he convinced them that he was a genuine F.B.I. agent looking for me, so they let me go in his custody. I'll have to give Longh a bonus in his next paycheck.

Once I got into the car, I found out that Longh had been busy, too.

"Study this carefully, Dakota," he said, handing me a photograph of the other side of the mountain. At first glance it just looked like a large boulder with some scrub brush scattered at its base.

"Not very exciting, Longh. I hope you don't plan to enter this in any photo contest," I said.

"No. No. Take a closer look," he said, pulling out a large magnifying glass. "Look at the shadows down here. They mark the opening of two caves in the back side of the mountain. Sacred caves."

I squinted and looked more closely. There they were. "They look like two upside down U's."

"That's where you can get inside. A kind of back door. The Indian chief's son took this picture for me," Longh said.

"But none of this was on Viktor Herbert's map," I said. "Either he didn't know about these caves . . ."

"Or he did not want you to know about them," said Longh, finishing my sentence. "I think it is time to investigate Dr. Herbert, Dakota."

"Right, Longh. I want you to go and talk to whomever you can find at Getaway Plane Rentals, the outfit that owned the clunker we saw crash in the woods. I'm going to head out to Jungle Ed's place to see what he can tell me. Meet me out there when you're finished."

Thanks to a wild rainstorm, the drive to Ed's took longer than usual. When I got there, no one was in the trailer, and the only signs of life were his snakes hissing and crawling around in their cages. It was such a miserable night I even felt sorry for the snakes. Using my well-developed lock-picking abilities, I managed to pop the lock to Ed's office, if you could call it that.

As soon as I stepped inside, I saw that the place was cleaned out. Ed was a pretty thorough packer, judging by the emptiness of his closet and dresser. The only things left behind: his sweat-stained hat with its fake leopardskin band and a **book of matches**.

I was getting ready to move out of the room when I saw a shadow move across one of the windows. Whoever it was moved like a cat. And he didn't want to be seen. I slipped off my moccasins and eased over to the side of the door. The visitor stepped into the doorway and carefully scanned the room. He knew what he was doing. He didn't want to be surprised. But as I learned from my years of training as a magician, people look where they are used to looking: straight ahead, to the side, and

sometimes up. But never down—unless something draws their attention there.

I was as still as a stone as the intruder stepped into the room. When he paused, I reached out and grabbed his ankles from behind. I was about to pull his feet out from under him when I heard a familiar voice: "Dakota! No! It is I, Longh."

"Longh!" I exclaimed. "How did you get through with your work at the airport so fast?"

"Simple. The airport was closed. I will have to go back later."

"Well, you didn't miss any party here either. It looks as if Ed skipped town. We saw it coming, but we had nothing solid to pin on him."

Longh scanned the room. "He did not leave much. Except for the snakes. Make certain they are all in their cages. I did not bring my snakebite kit."

"I think we're safe. Look what I've found." I showed him the matches.

"Bring them on our next camping trip, Dakota. Maybe then you will be able to start a fire without your lighter."

I let that one go by.

"No, Longh. These could mean something. The rest of the office was picked clean. Ed must have dropped them. The cover is still clean and inside there's some writing. **A number: 900,000 divided by 10 with the result—90,000—and then the amount $45,000 and an address in Hawaii.** And there is one more thing, **all the missing matches are from the left side of the match-book.** You know what <u>that</u> means?"

CLUE #8

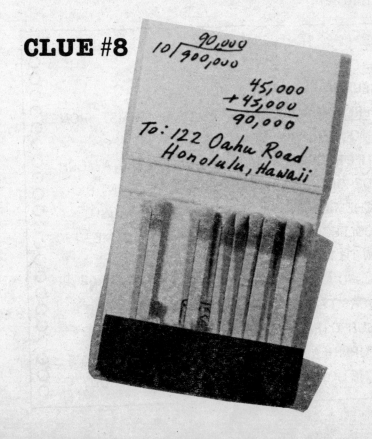

"Whoever was using these matches was left-handed," Longh observed, "unlike Jungle Ed."

"This lefty must have been working with our friend, Jungle Ed, on something involving big sums of money. There's a southpaw scientist I'd like to check out next."

I picked up Ed's phone and called Zan's answering machine. "Zan, this is Tarzan. One last request: get me what you can on Dr. Viktor Herbert, a government scientist at Iron Mountain. Thanks."

By the time Longh and I got home back to our base camp office there was a note on the computer bulletin board that there was a message waiting. Sure enough, it was from Zan:

COMPUTER REPORT

SUBJECT: VICKTOR HERBERT.

PRESENT OCCUPATION: SENIOR SCIENTIST, IRON MOUNTAIN LABORATORY.

LIFE HISTORY: WORLD WAR TWO HERO—A MUCH DECORATED PARATROOPER. A BRILLIANT BIO-CHEMIST AND GENETIC ENGINEER. TAUGHT COLLEGE FOR YEARS AND WHEN HE CAME UP WITH THE SPECIAL ENHANCING FORMULA USED AT IRON MOUNTAIN HE QUIT THE UNI-VERSITY TO START HIS OWN BUSINESS AND SUPPOSEDLY MAKE MILLIONS SELLING HIS FORMULA TO THE GOVERNMENT. HOWEVER, THE GOVERNMENT DECLARED HIS METHOD

TOP SECRET, TOOK IT OVER, AND PUT HIM TO WORK AT IRON MOUNTAIN. HE DIDN'T GET A DIME. RUMOR HAS IT HE WASN'T TOO PLEASED ABOUT IT, BUT I'M TOLD THEY MADE IT WORTH HIS WHILE. JUST RECENTLY HE HIRED LUCILLE DORMAN TO WORK IN HIS LAB. SHORTLY AFTER THAT, THE BLACK FANG STUFF STARTED TO DISAPPEAR.

HOBBIES, INTERESTS: LIKES TO GO OUT **HIKING, STUDIES INDIAN TRIBAL RITUALS.** LAST YEAR BOUGHT A SMALL PIECE OF A SOUTH PACIFIC ISLAND.

IN ALL, PRETTY DULL AND NOT A REAL EXCITING SUSPECT. I'M NOT INVITING HIM TO MY NEXT PARTY.

LOVE AND XXXXX'S TO ALL (EXTRA XXX'S TO YOU, TARZAN).

—ZAN

END OF REPORT

"Alexandra is correct," said Longh. "Dr. Herbert sounds too ordinary to seek revenge."

"True. But even dullards can be crooks. This means that it's time to go back to Iron Mountain. Meet me by the jeep in forty-five minutes in your Ninja suit."

"Ninja suit? What are we going to be doing, Dakota?"

"Nothing that we want to be recognized for," I said.

Curious but calm as always, Longh collected his clothes as I got the rest of our gear: the heavy-duty climbing ropes, the knapsacks, climbing harnesses—nylon straps through which we hooked our climbing ropes, and special sponge-soled climbing boots to help us walk over the slippery rock.

Once the jeep was loaded, Longh and I headed back out into the desert, toward the Indian reservation. I remembered from my childhood days on the reservation that a night like this, with a full moon, was considered magical.

It was a long night. First we had to find the medicine man. We went from house to house on the reservation, looking for him. At first no one admitted to knowing there even was a medicine man, but once I began speaking to them in their own dialect, which I had learned as a small boy, they became more friendly. Many houses later, we managed to find him, tending to a sick child.

Ordinarily, Indians that important don't talk to just anyone. Fortunately, I was prepared for the meeting. I showed him the tattoo on the inside of my wrist—a small eagle in flight. Only to a few did it mean anything, namely, that I had been initiated into the inner realm of spiritual guides—mystically trained Indian braves. It was the first step to becoming a medicine man.

When he saw the tattoo, the medicine man nodded silently in recognition. He was an old man with skin the color of smoked wood. His hair was gray and frizzled, and his eyes shone with an inner light. Quickly, using his language, I explained we were trying to find a poison, one which could endanger his tribe and many other people if it were released accidentally. He looked directly at me and spoke. I clicked my watch on:

****

TRANSCRIPT

MM: THERE'S NO NEED TO TALK IN DIALECT. I SPEAK PERFECTLY GOOD ENGLISH, YOU KNOW. I'M A GRADUATE OF HARVARD.

DK: YOU KNOW ABOUT THE WORK AT IRON MOUNTAIN, THEN?

MM: YES, OF COURSE. THEY THINK WE DUMB INDIANS DON'T KNOW WHAT THEY'RE DOING THERE.

DK: A SHORT TIME AGO SOME DANGEROUS...

LG: <u>VERY</u> DANGEROUS, INDEED...

DK: YES, VERY DANGEROUS MATERIAL WAS STOLEN FROM THERE, AND WE'RE TRYING TO LOCATE IT. WE THINK YOU CAN HELP US.

MM: I'LL DO WHAT I CAN. WHAT IS IT YOU NEED TO KNOW?

DK: THOSE CAVES HIGH UP ON THIS SIDE OF THE MOUNTAIN—THEY APPEAR TO BE THE PERFECT SITE FOR SACRED BURIALS. IS THAT TRUE?

MM: MANY YEARS AGO OUR TRIBE DID BURY THEIR TRIBESMEN THERE. THE CAVE OPENINGS FACE THE RAYS OF THE SETTING SUN.

DK: IS THAT TRADITION STILL FOLLOWED?

MM: THOSE ARE ANCIENT CUSTOMS, MR. KING. I AM A MODERN INDIAN.

DK: I DIDN'T ASK THAT. I ASKED IF YOU STILL GO THERE AND HONOR THOSE CUSTOMS.

MM: YES, I DO. THERE ARE THOSE AMONG US WHO STILL BELIEVE IN THE SACREDNESS OF THE MOUNTAIN, EVEN IF THE SCIENTISTS ON THE OTHER SIDE DO

NOT. WE NO LONGER BURY OUR BRAVES THERE, BUT WE DO HONOR THAT TRADITION BY LAYING **A SMALL CEREMONIAL FIGURE** THERE AS A GIFT TO THE PERSON WHO HAS DIED.

DK: [AT THIS POINT I EXCITEDLY GRABBED A COPY OF THE SKETCH I HAD MADE OF HERBERT'S INDIAN DOLL.] DID THE FIGURE LOOK LIKE THIS?

MM: WHY, YES.

DK: WHO KNOWS THOSE CAVES?

MM: I DO. AND OF COURSE MY SON.

DK: IS HE AROUND?

MM: ORDINARILY HE WOULD BE, BUT NOT TONIGHT. HE'S A STATE POLICE OFFICER. HE AND THE OTHER OFFICERS HAVE BEEN MOBILIZED TO LOCATE AN INTRUDER WHO GOT AWAY FROM THE SECURITY FORCES AT THE LAB EARLIER TODAY. [HMMM . . . GUESS THAT WAS ME!]

DK: WHAT I WANT TO KNOW IS, HOW FAR INTO THE MOUNTAIN DO THOSE CAVES GO?

MM: ALL THE WAY, IF YOU HAVE THE TIME AND THE COURAGE TO EXPLORE THEM.

DK: IN OTHER WORDS, I COULD GO STRAIGHT THROUGH TO THE OTHER SIDE IF I WANTED?

MM: I KNOW WHAT YOU ARE THINKING, MR. K. YES, THERE ONCE WAS A LONG TUNNEL THAT BURROWED STRAIGHT THROUGH THE MOUNTAIN. NOW IT ENDS AT THE LAB COMPLEX. BUT GETTING THROUGH THE TUNNEL IS NOT AS EASY AS IT SOUNDS. MY SON AND I, ALONG WITH SOME OTHER TRIBESMEN, SEALED THAT UP A LONG TIME AGO.

DK: DID THE GOVERNMENT PEOPLE EVER FIND OUT ABOUT IT?

MM: NOT THAT I KNOW OF.

DK: DIDN'T YOU TELL THEM?

MM: NO.

DK: WHY NOT?

MM: THEY NEVER ASKED. AND BESIDES, IF THEY KNEW, THEY WOULD HAVE KEPT US FROM USING OUR SACRED MOUNTAIN. WE COULDN'T HAVE THAT. SO ONLY OUR TRIBE—AND WHOEVER ELSE HAS BEEN SHREWD ENOUGH TO FIGURE IT OUT—HAVE KNOWN OF THE CAVE COMPLEX.

END OF TRANSCRIPT

****

Dakota King's
Microdiary Entry #11
Re: <u>Operation Black Fang</u>

I asked the medicine man to draw me a map of the cave complex showing where the long tunnel was.

"It starts with a large open mouth," said the chief. "As you move back the passageway gets narrower and narrower. Eventually you come to a wall of boulders. Look for the one with the snake painted on it. That is the keystone. Take that one out, and the others will be easy to remove."

"It looks simple enough," said Longh.

"Do not be careless," the Indian warned. "It is not simple. It takes an experienced cave explorer to find his way around. You will see the skeletons of those who got lost. So be careful. And watch out for the spirits of the mountain."

At dawn the next morning, Longh and I were in my jeep, headed for the mountain. In a few minutes we reached the foot of it. We looked up at the huge stretch of stone that towered over us. We unloaded our climbing gear, loaded it on our shoulders, and began the climb.

We started by using footholds that had been carved there centuries ago by Indian climbers. In a couple of hours we had reached the mouth of one of the caves, the one that went all the way into the mountain. At first it was simple to make our way through the passageway. But after a while it got narrower and narrower, just as the medicine man said it would. The ceiling kept making us duck our heads lower, until finally we were crawling along on our hands and knees. By that time we had turned on our headlamps. As I crawled along, I turned and my light picked up a little color on the rocks. It looked like **flakes of green paint.**

The passageway came to an end—or it seemed to—in a small room where we could stand up. Directly in front of us was a wall of boulders with animal drawings on them. Some were birds. Some were lizards. Only one boulder had a snake painted on it. Longh and I struggled to lift it out, only to find a wall of smaller boulders behind it. After removing these, we finally found the tunnel the medicine man had told us about.

We followed it for a few dozen yards until it ended at what looked like a slab of wood. I leaned against it and pushed hard. Nothing happened. Longh silently signaled by flashing his light at me and then pointing it at a huge steel ring attached to the wall. He and I grabbed it and pulled. Slowly it swung toward us.

I shone my light into the dark chamber behind it and saw . . . the closet where I had had my battle with the snake!

I signaled to Longh in sign language, in which we were both fluent: "I'll bet that whoever let that snake loose on me slipped out this way."

"And whoever stole the poison probably transported it out this way as well," Longh signaled back.

Slowly, he and I made our way into the room. We opened the door a crack and peered out into the corridor. The coast was clear. We slipped out the door, staying in the shadows as much as possible. We decided to have a look at Viktor Herbert's office first, since his was the closest. Then we would check Lucille Dorman's to see if there were any interesting clues.

The laboratory was dimly lit at night, perfect camouflage for our black Ninja uniforms. Staying close to the walls, Longh and I made our way down the corridor, rounded a corner, and almost crashed into a sentry who, fortunately, was standing there with his back to us. To be more accurate, he was leaning against the wall, dozing.

The sentry yawned, stretched his arms, and picked up the automatic rifle leaning against the wall. He raised his head. I used my old Ninja trick of studying the muscles in the base of his neck to figure out where he was looking. I could tell his eyes were sweeping the corridor. I guessed he was getting ready to go. I signaled to Longh it was time for both of us to move.

Years ago I had learned how to perform the eighty-one special moves of Pi Mi Hsing Tung, the Ninja Art of Stealth. These were developed by a tribe of warrior monks who lived in the mountains of Tibet and who taught me many of the moves. Much later, when I lived in Japan, I was a student in special midnight classes in Inpo, the skill of sneaking into an enemy's camp. That's where I met Longh—he was there to improve his skills. We wore special training suits with bells on them, and we had to walk across a field of loose stones on a moonless night without stumbling and without making the bells jingle. Longh and I were at the head of the class in this skill, which was certainly coming in handy now at Iron Mountain.

The guard had shifted his position but did not actually move. Because the Ninja is never to be seen unless he chooses to be, we melted into the shadows. Then, finally, the soldier stepped away from the wall and began to turn in our direction. At the same time we moved slowly along the wall to stay right behind the guard as he turned. Finally, when he had made a complete circle, we were still standing directly behind him. I held my breath, waiting for him to take a step, but he didn't.

Ninjas rely on the art of illusion. Now was the time for a very simple one. I carried in my left breast pocket a half dozen or so small glass disks. They are light and easy to pack and, when thrown or rolled along a floor, make a wonderfully mysterious noise. When they hit, they shatter into such small pieces they leave no clues behind.

Carefully—and silently—I lobbed one of those disks past the sentry in the direction we had just come from. A sharp tinkling noise sounded in the darkness, far down the corridor. Instantly the soldier's head snapped up. He headed away from us, toward the sound. Longh and I waited until he was out of sight. Then we each took a deep breath and carefully moved along the corridor, in the other direction.

In a minute or so we were at the door to Viktor Herbert's office. It was locked, but that was no problem. In about fifteen seconds we had the door open, and we were inside. Whoever had been in there was in a hurry to find something. The place was a shambles, and it was hard to tell if anything had been taken. I made a mental note of the room and sketched it later.

While I searched the level of the room high, Longh checked the room low. He examined the wastebasket. "One can tell more about a person by what he throws away than what he keeps," Longh said as I mouthed the very same words. Longh says that exact thing every time we go rummaging through people's garbage. Finally, down near the bottom of the wastebasket, he struck it rich. There in his hand was an **empty book of matches from the Bamboo Garden Restaurant.** Whoever our thief was had a yen for Chinese food.

"Interesting," Longh said.

"Yeah, and maybe these were deliberately planted here by someone else," I added. "Why don't we go down the hall and check out Lucille Dorman's office?"

CLUE #9

We slipped out the door, locking it behind us, and picked the lock on Lucille Dorman's office. Compared to Herbert's, hers was neat as a pin. We split up our search again, and in a few seconds Longh whistled quietly and said, "Dakota!" He pointed at a spot under Lucille Dorman's desk. I aimed my flashlight there, and it shone on a **strange-looking bottle with a red label stuck on the outside. Printed across the label in large black letters was: UPS474.**

CLUE #10

"Take a photograph, Dakota," Longh said. I whipped out my belt-buckle camera and took a couple of quick snapshots. We searched the rest of the office, but found nothing else incriminating. We opened the door a slit and peered out into the hallway. All seemed dim and quiet, so we eased our bodies into the corridor, staying as close to the wall as possible and moving sideways with the special crossover Ninja step. A few more turns later we were nearing the supply closet where we came in from the tunnel. Longh was just moving toward the door when there was an explosion of noise. Sirens wailing. Voices shouting. A repeated warning coming over the speakers in the ceiling above our head: "ATTENTION SECURITY. ATTENTION SECURITY. RED ALERT. RED ALERT. CLASSIFIED MATERIAL MISSING. THIS IS NOT A DRILL. SEAL OFF THE MOUNTAIN AND MOVE TO YOUR RED ALERT POSITIONS. I REPEAT. THIS IS NOT A DRILL. RED ALERT. RED ALERT . . ." The sirens screamed louder and louder. Longh and I looked at each other. We knew we must have tripped a silent alarm in one of the offices.

In almost the same instant, a group of blinding lights blinked on. Every nook and cranny of the place was lit, and the sentry cameras were aimed everywhere. At the same time the motion sensors under the floors were turned on. A camera down the hall came alive. We could hear its humming motor as it slowly started to sweep back and forth across the area. I knew we had two, maybe three, seconds to do something.

Longh lunged for the doorknob. Locked. There was no time to pick the lock. We raced across the hall and stood directly underneath the camera as it made its sweeps. The camera couldn't see us, but we were trapped there. I knew we couldn't cut the camera wires without triggering another alarm. I pulled some black electrician's tape out of my pocket and, with my knife, cut off a piece of black fabric from my Ninja uniform. Longh figured out right away what the plan was. I handed him the tape and cloth and hoisted him up on my shoulders. Without disturbing the camera's motion, Longh put the black cloth over the lens and taped it in place. We hoped it would be a while before anyone noticed this camera was blind.

The next problem was to get across the corridor without touching the floor and setting off more sensors. I had another idea. There was a door behind us that was opposite the closet door across the hall. I took off my coil of climbing rope and made a loop in the end. After two tries I managed to lasso the closet doorknob. I pulled tight and tied my end of the rope around the doorknob behind us. In a few seconds I had a tightrope stretching from doorknob to doorknob across the corridor. Longh watched me intently.

"I'm going to show you what I learned when I worked in a gypsy circus," I told him. With a steadying hand from Longh, I climbed up on the tightrope and began a quick rope walk across the hall. The rope was wiggly, and I had a hard time keeping my balance. But I made it.

Once I got to the other side, I managed to pop the lock. Longh came across the rope, more shakily than I. I had used a special slipknot I knew from magician's training. Two sharp tugs, and the rope was free.

Longh coiled up the rope. "Okay, Dakota. Let's go." Longh turned, and as he did, something dropped from his rucksack onto the center of the floor with all its sensors. Alarms went off. Guards came running. But by the time the first sentry arrived, all he saw were two closed doors and a sentry camera with black cloth taped over its lens. We had already gone through the other door leading out of the closet and slipped back into the tunnel.

We made our way through the darkness as fast as we could. Neither Long nor I knew whether the guards were aware of the back passage, and we weren't about to wait and find out. We ran fast, sometimes stumbling over the stones in our way.

I was running ahead when I heard a noise. I turned just in time to see some sort of creature with giant eyes step out of the shadows and whack Longh on the back of his neck. He went down. Whoever, or whatever, it was came running toward me in a crouch. I reached into my rucksack and pulled out my camera. I knew that in that dark tunnel the flash would be blinding. I pressed the button, and in a millisecond there was a blast of bright white light.

I took advantage of my attacker's temporary blindness and jumped behind some large boulders. Once his vision cleared, he prowled around, looking for me. He stepped in front of where I was hiding when Longh came to. The soldier turned. His back was to me, so I made my move.

But as I scrambled from my hiding place, the masked soldier instantly turned and grabbed my arm in a crushing grip with his left hand. I saw him raise his right hand to give me a karate chop. In an instant, I remembered what my Ninja master told me about hand-to-hand combat: "In every moment of violence there is force flowing around you. Try to be one with that force, and victory will be yours."

This time the only force I could use was that of me falling down. So I deliberately fell down again, pulling the soldier off balance. He toppled forward. His helmeted head went <u>clunk</u> against the cave wall. Before he could get up, I had his arms pinned down. Longh had

come over to help.

He pulled off the soldier's helmet and mask. I clicked on the flashlight. The soldier held up his hands to protect his eyes from the bright light. I pulled them back down and there, staring back at us, was Lucille Dorman!

At that point, Boss, Longh and I tied Ms. Dorman's hands with our rope and led her down the mountain passageway. With our flashlights we scanned every inch of the passageway walls.

Finally we spotted something—a crack in the rock we hadn't noticed on the way in. Again, using a Ninja trick, I managed to slip through the narrow slit. I pulled Ms. Dorman through after me, all ninety-five furious pounds of her. Then Longh came through like the lean animal he is.

We were in yet another passageway. We inched along until Longh pointed his flashlight toward something—a **fleck of green paint** on the rock. We followed the small passage until it ended against a slab of heavy wood. I scanned its surface with my flashlight beam and saw a small button on the right-hand side. I pushed it. There was a soft click. Slowly the panel swung away. We saw that this hidden passage led into a room. On the other side of the panel was a bookcase. The minute I saw the room, which was **in a shambles,** I knew who our villain was. Longh and I turned to look at Ms. Dorman. She said nothing, but stood there, staring into the room.

The thief had to be one of three people: Jungle Ed, Viktor Herbert, or Lucille Dorman. After examining all the clues, I could see that these three each had the abilities needed to pull off the theft. Whoever stole the venom had to be able to fly a plane (or get someone who could), had to have the skill to parachute out of it, and have an insider's knowledge of the Iron Mountain complex—maybe even knowledge of the Indian caves. That person also had to have a reason for the theft. What could it be—money, revenge, part of some evil master plan?

No question in my mind now. I knew the identity of the villain who had stolen the deadly snake venom. All the clues came together.

That night I assembled this file for you, Boss. I want to see if you can put the clues together and figure out, as I did, who the thief was. Why don't I just tell you? Hey, Boss, I don't want to spoil all the fun for you, right? That's just the kind of guy I am.

Anyway, I'm off for a swinging time in the jungle. I'll mail you the answer to this mystery from there. But for now, **I'm outta here, Boss!**

FROM:
DAKOTA KING
SOUTH AMERICA

TO:
ZONE OPERATIONS ORGANIZATION
9909 INCOGNITO DRIVE
ARLINGTON, VIRGINIA 90909

I'm outta here, Boss!

DK

And The Villain Is . . .

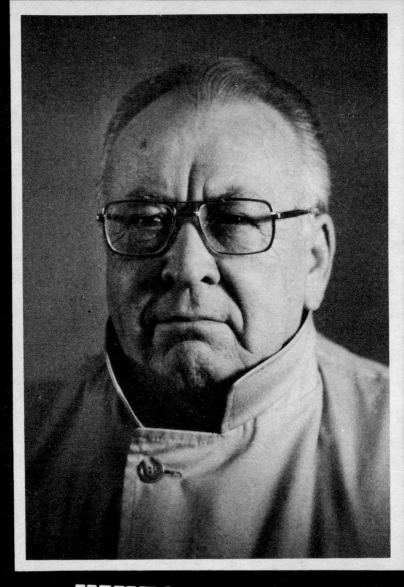

. . . . . **VIKTOR HERBERT**

There were a few things about him that didn't make sense. One was that, for someone who claimed to have been hiking recently, it didn't make sense that he had a serious breathing problem. His colleagues all said he was using his oxygen tank more than ever. Secondly, for someone who had lost the opportunity to make millions of dollars from his secret process, he didn't act very annoyed at the government. Almost anyone would have been a little upset about what had happened to him.

Little by little, Boss, the pieces fell together. For one thing, when I was in his office I noticed that in the photo on his shelf, his uniform had a set of pilot's wings. Now don't forget the plane that went down in the woods was an old clunker, one that an old pilot, even one who hadn't flown in years, would know how to fly.

And then there was that left glove. Herbert was a left-hander. In order to pull the ripcord of the parachute, he must have gotten rid of the glove just before opening the plane door, which is why it ended up being stuck in the door handle.

As for that doll on his shelf, the medicine man had said that my sketch of it looked like their sacred ceremonial figure. Only someone intimately familiar with the Indian caves would have found one or even known where to look. And don't forget, he was an expert in Indian lore. Finally, there were those metal oxygen tanks painted green.

But before I get to those, let me talk about the security in the laboratory. There was only one way in and out of that mountain. Or so everyone thought. Even if you were an authorized person, getting any of that forbidden lab material past all those guards and detectors seemed impossible. First, the thief had to find another way out—a back way. And Herbert did—quite a while ago, probably—during one of his hikes. He knew about the legend of the burial caves and explored far enough to know they went all the way through. Over time, he cleared the rocks to make a passage for himself (and along the way grabbed one of the ceremonial dolls for himself, greedy man).

Next he had to figure out a way to steal the poison and package it. Everything he was working with was extremely dangerous if not handled correctly. He needed a fail-safe container. That's when he got his next brainstorm: his phony breathing problem. By getting clearance from security, he was able to bring in his oxygen tanks. In time, people got used to seeing him walking around with an oxygen tank trailing behind him.

It was a simple matter to drain the tanks and refill them with UPS474. Dr. Herbert was well known in his own labs. Even the guards watching the television monitor wouldn't watch him for very long. With a little sleight-of-hand and a lot of care, he was able to slip a container of the supervenom inside a tank during a lab visit and stroll away with it.

During a quiet time at night, he was able to slip a tank out through the secret opening he had made behind his bookcase, leading into the narrow passage that connected his office to the old Indian caves. I'll bet on every one of his hikes he went inside, took a green metal oxygen canister, and dragged it to the mouth of the cave where he hid it with the others he had collected—we found green paint scrapings all over the place.

Longh took photos of all our suspects to Getaway Plane Rentals, where they identified Jungle Ed as the guy who'd rented that junk airplane. Herbert must have blackmailed him. (Ex-convicts aren't supposed to be doing business with such a top-secret lab.) Herbert then flew the plane to the desert behind the mountain and loaded a sample canister in the back. Once in flight, he wedged the Y-shaped stick behind the controls to make the plane fly on and bailed out with his canister of poison. (I'll bet he sprained his ankle in the jump.) In such a remote area, who would be around to notice either the plane or the parachutist?

To get a little revenge on Lucille Dorman (she did develop the method that Herbert took credit for) and distract attention from himself, he took the venom from her section, not expecting she would be able to replace it so soon. He then tried to make her look guilty by sending the threatening note to the plane rental guy on her stationery. He also put those empty containers under her desk and messed up his own office to make it look as though someone had stolen something from him.

Herbert's plan was risky, and it almost paid off. Someone was probably waiting for him on the ground and no doubt would have given him a nice pile of money for his efforts. I would guess, judging by the figures on the matchbook cover, about $900,000, some of which he promised to pay to Jungle Ed. I think, Boss, if you check Dr. Herbert's bank account, you might find that he has some of that advance money there. Some of that probably went for a one-way plane ticket for the plane rental agent. The money came from some foreign spies trying to buy better weapons for their government, a plot foiled by Disappearing Inc.—yours truly, that is, Boss.

So Herbert spent all these years biding his time, preparing to get even with the government. He even picked out his own island to retire to. Unfortunately, Dr. Herbert will not be spending his retirement on his island. Where he's going he won't be needing all that money he was going to sock away—the government will be providing him with everything he needs, including a set of bars on the window.

Dakota King

CASE CLOSED

"I'm outta here, Boss!"

DISAPPEARING INC.

DAKOTA KING
AGENT AT LARGE

Congratulations!

You've solved the case of <u>Operation: Black Fang</u>! But that is just the beginning and is only the first file in <u>The Secret Files of Dakota King</u> series.

Now that you've proven yourself to be a case-cracker of the highest quality, you're ready to dig into the other <u>Secret Files of Dakota King</u>. You are requested to join the secret agents at Zone Operations Organization (also known as the Z.O.O.), and help them solve the unsolved cases left behind by that always-on-the-go, agent-at-large, Dakota King. King and Longh Gonh, his partner at Disappearing Inc., are off on yet another exciting adventure. The results of their travels are always the same—files full of clues, transcripts, maps, scraps of paper, sketches, photographs, and who knows what else. Are you ready to face the next case?

Get some rest and plenty of it (you deserve it after <u>Operation: Black Fang</u>!). Then get set to tackle more <u>Secret Files of Dakota King</u>. Dakota, Longh, the Zoo-keeper . . . they're *all* counting on YOU!

THE SECRET FILES OF
DAKOTA KING

#2 The Haunted City of Gold

Jake MacKenzie

There's a treasure missing and everybody's after it!

Poisoned darts, flying double-edged daggers, haunted statues, and deadly tarantulas make just another day in the jungle just another brush with death for Dakota King and his partner Longh Gonh.

Somewhere deep in the jungles of Paramar, a treasure lost for centuries lies undiscovered. But where? It's King's job to find it, and as his search begins, he quickly discovers that he's not the only one on this treasure hunt! Whoever it is that's on the jungle trail to the treasure wants to make sure that Dakota King never makes it out of this jungle alive.

What is the treasure? Where is it hidden? Who else is after it? And most important of all, will Dakota King get out of this mess in one piece? All the answers are here in The Haunted City of Gold, file #2 of The Secret Files of Dakota King.

THE SECRET FILES OF
DAKOTA KING

#3 Two-Wheeled Terror

Jake MacKenzie

A boy, a bicycle, and somebody's following them both!

Alex Walker's slick, new, foreign racing bike arrives on time, and with it comes big trouble! Strangers start following Alex, his bike is stolen, and he's caught in the middle of a mysterious mess only Dakota King can untangle.

Why would anyone want to steal his bike? Who are the unknown drivers of the fancy BMW car that shows up wherever Alex is? Who is that interesting pipe-smoking man with the English accent? Why is the bike shop owner suddenly so nervous?

Dakota King and Longh Gonh allow Alex to work with them to find clues for this file as all three train for an important bike race. On the track of clues and on the race track, they're a team determined to discover who's responsible for the Two-Wheeled Terror, file #3 of The Secret Files of Dakota King.

THE SECRET FILES OF
DAKOTA KING

#4 Secrets of the Lost Mine

Jake MacKenzie

**All that glitters is not gold . . .
sometimes it's a ghost!**

Where is Zeb Ingalls? Dakota King
returns to the town he knew as a boy
and discovers that his good friend Zeb
has mysteriously disappeared! It all
seems suspicious since Zeb has just sold
his land with a gold mine on it to a
group of real estate developers from the
city. Who would want to hurt Zeb?

In his search for his friend, Dakota
King stumbles onto a story about a
miner driven mad by the powers of the
mine. And, when he reaches the old
mine himself, spirits from the past
reveal themselves to King, while evil
from the present threatens to keep him
from finding the answers he's looking
for. Ghosts, attacks in the night, and a
treasure more valuable than gold fill this
file full of clues to help YOU discover the
Secrets of the Lost Mine, file #4 of The
Secret Files of Dakota King.